The Summer I Met My Mom

K.S. DeLuca

Her whole world shifted in one name.
"DeLuca," she whispered. "Scarlet DeLuca."
By K.S. DeLuca

Acknowledgements

I'd like to thank my family and friends for giving me the kind of neighborhood memories that still make me smile.

To everyone I grew up with-thank you for the laughter, the loyalty, and the late summer nights that inspired every page of this book.

And to Fredo, who supports every crazy idea I have.

~ To Samantha for the inspo
~ and to my high school English teacher who didn't believe
in me, this one is for you, wherever you are…

Contents

Chapter One

The Closet

Scarlet DeLuca had lived in Princeton for as long as she could remember, but it never quite felt like home. Her mom, Melissa Russo, always said they were lucky—to live in a good neighborhood, to go to good schools. But lately, all Scarlet could see was how little they understood each other.

At seventeen, Scarlet was elegant, composed, and often called "mature for her age." She read classic novels, corrected people's grammar under her breath, and preferred black coffee over caramel Frappuccinos. But nothing made her feel more like a stranger in her own house than trying to talk to her mom.

Melissa was loud. She filled every room with energy, stories, and opinions. She was a single mom who ran her own salon, had a flair for leopard prints, and never met a topic she didn't have something to say about. To Scarlet, she was exhausting. To Melissa, Scarlet was too quiet, too serious, too... not like her.

That summer had already been long. Scarlet spent most of it avoiding conversations, walking the quiet streets of their Princeton neighborhood with earbuds in, rereading

Wuthering Heights, and trying not to let her mom's constant talking get under her skin.

They had argued the night before over something stupid—laundry or college or the fact that Melissa didn't knock before entering her room. Scarlet slammed the door, Melissa shouted something through it, and that was that.

Now, Scarlet stood in Melissa's walk-in closet, an untouched cup of cold coffee in her hand, staring at a dusty box marked "Missy – High School." Missy. That was what everyone used to call her mom. Somehow, seeing the name written in faded marker felt like looking at a "stranger things" episode.

She set the coffee down and opened the box.

Inside were old pictures—Polaroids with dates scrawled in black Sharpie, ticket stubs, yearbooks, a flattened corsage. She picked up a photo: a blonde girl with thin brows and brown-lined lips, wearing a spaghetti strap top and throwing up a peace sign. There was something wild and fun in her expression—something Scarlet didn't recognize in the woman currently doing inventory at the salon and texting her constantly.

She turned the Polaroid over. In loopy handwriting, it read: Missy – August 1996.

Scarlet smiled faintly and leaned back, still holding the photo. Her head tapped gently against the edge of the open closet shelf.

That's when everything tilted.

The room spun—no, the closet spun—faster than she could process. She shut her eyes and instinctively reached out, expecting to hit hangers or the wall, but felt only air. The scent of her mom's perfume was replaced by something entirely different: Sun-In, salty air, and strawberry Lip Smackers.

When she opened her eyes, she was lying on the floor. But it wasn't her mom's walk-in closet anymore.

It was a bedroom. A tiny one, with a floral bedspread, cassette tapes on the dresser, and a poster of Leonardo DiCaprio thumbtacked to the wall.

Scarlet blinked. Sat up.

She was definitely not in her mom's closet anymore. Definitely not in 2025 anymore.

Footsteps approached in the hallway. A girl's voice called out, "Ma, have you seen my—"

The door creaked open.

And there, in the doorway, stood the girl from the Polaroid. Blonde, thin-browed, all lip liner and attitude.

She looked at Scarlet and blinked. "Uh... what the hell?"

Scarlet scrambled to her feet. "I— I can explain," she said, though she couldn't.

Missy narrowed her eyes. "Who are you??!!" Are you like... and what are you doing in my room?"

Scarlet clutched the photo to her chest and searched for words. None came.

Missy tilted her head. "You okay?"

"I... think I hit my head," Scarlet managed, her voice small. "I'm not sure how I got here."

Missy glanced down the hall, then back at Scarlet. Something flickered in her expression— not suspicion, not fear. Just curiosity. "Well... you don't look like a burglar."

Scarlet smiled weakly.

Missy grinned. "You're lucky I'm so trusting. C'mon, you can hang out here till you figure it out.

What's your name, anyway?"

Scarlet hesitated. "Carli," she said. The name slipped out before she could stop it.

Missy nodded slowly. "Carli, huh? Cool. I'm Missy."

Scarlet looked at the girl—her mom, as a teenager. And for the first time in a long time, she felt something unexpected.

She felt at home.

Chapter Two

Bacon

The kitchen smelled like bacon grease, hairspray, and something sweet—fabric softener, maybe. The radio on the counter played softly through static: "Give Me One Reason" by Tracy Chapman, the chords warm and familiar.

Scarlet hovered awkwardly by the doorway, stomach flipping. This wasn't just someone's house. It was her mom's house. Except it was her mom before she was a mom—before PTA meetings, before takeout on busy nights, before everything got complicated.

Missy grabbed a pan from the stove with her bare hand, swearing under her breath. "Damn it, that's hot."

Scarlet flinched at the sharp noise. Everything here felt louder, brighter, too real.

A woman's voice called from another room, sharp and Staten Island strong, "Missy! Garbage!"

"Ma! Later!" Missy shouted, rolling her eyes dramatically. "She's so annoying," she muttered, smirking at Scarlet like they were already friends sharing secrets. She opened the fridge and pulled out a carton of orange juice, sipping straight from it.

Scarlet didn't move. She felt like if she breathed too hard, the whole place might dissolve like a dream.

Missy gave her a look. "You just gonna stand there or what?"

Scarlet opened her mouth. Closed it again. Finally, she said, "so I think I hit my head."

Missy blinked. "You what?"

"I was—I don't even know. I was somewhere else, and... I was looking at these pictures, and then... I hit my head. And now I'm here." Scarlet pressed her fingers to her temple, like she could rub the truth out of it.

Missy stared at her like she was trying to decide if Scarlet was crazy or just weird. But then something softened in her expression. "That's rough."

Scarlet nodded miserably.

Missy folded her arms, biting her lip in thought. "Well... you don't look like a psycho."

Scarlet looked down at herself. Tank top. Jeans. Converse. Nothing threatening, just out of place.

"I don't know what's going on," Scarlet admitted, voice quieter now. "I'm not trying to mess anything up. I'm just... really confused."

Missy studied her a little longer. "You from Jersey?"

Scarlet nodded. "Princeton."

Missy made a face like she wasn't sure whether that was impressive or lame. "Figures. You talk kinda fancy. Like a rich girl in a movie or something."

"I'm not rich," Scarlet said quickly. "I just... live there."

Missy leaned against the counter, squinting like she was reading something written across

Scarlet's forehead. "You know you're in Staten Island now. You got family out here or something?"

Scarlet hesitated. "Not really, I'm not sure, maybe." Scarlet didn't want to say.

For a second, the kitchen felt too quiet, like the whole house was waiting to see what Missy would decide.

Then she shrugged, like it wasn't a big deal after all. "Whatever. You can crash here until you get your head straight. My mom won't even notice. She's too busy screaming about garbage."

Scarlet blinked. "Really?"

"Yeah," Missy said, like it was obvious. "You seem nice. I'm a good judge of character."

Scarlet felt something ease in her chest at those words, even if they didn't make sense yet. Trust. Already. Just like that. Something deep in Missy knew too.

Missy grabbed two plates from the cabinet and plopped a couple slices of bacon on each.

"We'll figure it out. It's not like you robbed a store or something."

Scarlet sat down cautiously at the kitchen table. The vinyl seat squeaked under her.

"So... what's your name again?" Missy asked, plopping across from her.

Scarlet froze for a second. "Carli."

Missy gave a satisfied nod. "Cool name. I'm Missy, obviously."

Scarlet almost laughed. Obviously.

Missy pointed a greasy fork at her. "And don't worry, Carli from Princeton. You're with me now."

Scarlet managed a smile.

Missy grinned like she'd just adopted a stray kitten. "Anyway, summer's almost over. Soon it's gonna be school again. Uniforms, nuns yelling, blah blah blah." I go to St.

Veronica's. It's gonna be my senior year. Can't wait to be done."

Chapter Three

Breakfast Banter

The front steps of Missy's house were warm underfoot, even through Scarlet's sneakers. Somewhere down the block, sprinklers ticked rhythmically against a patchy lawn, and a lawnmower buzzed faintly in the distance.

Scarlet sat next to Missy on the stoop, both of them picking at the bacon they'd brought outside on paper towels.

"So," Missy said, squinting at her. "What's your deal, Carli?"

Scarlet chewed on her lip. She had no idea how to explain any of this. Not without sounding like she belonged in a padded room.

"I—I don't really know," she finally admitted. "I was in a bedroom looking through old pictures. And then I fell. I must've hit my head. And now I'm here."

Missy raised an eyebrow. "Like... here-here? Like in Staten Island?"

Scarlet shook her head. "No, yeah I mean... here. Like... your room. Your house."

Missy stared at her for a long second. "That is pretty weird."

"I know."

Missy didn't seem freaked out, though. More like... curious. She shrugged. "Well, if you're lost or whatever, we'll figure it out."

Scarlet glanced sideways at her. "Wow you are being so nice to me."

Missy made a face. "'Cause I'm not a jerk. And besides—" she nudged Scarlet with her shoulder "—I don't know. Something about you's familiar. I trust you. Don't make me regret it."

Scarlet gave a small smile. It was such a Missy answer, even though Missy didn't know it yet.

Fierce, loyal, a little bit reckless—but she followed her gut.

Scarlet tucked her knees up, arms wrapped around them. The street was quiet except for the hum of the summer day, that particular August feeling—summer break on its last legs, with school coming like a slow-moving wave in the distance.

Missy popped the last bite of bacon into her mouth and brushed her hands on her shorts.

"Anyway, you lucked out meeting me. I'm not even supposed to be home right now."

Scarlet blinked. "Where are you supposed to be?"

Missy rolled her eyes. "Out. Somewhere. Doesn't matter. My friends are probably gonna kill me when I tell 'em I met some random Jersey girl at my house instead of meeting up at Jess's."

"Jess?"

"Yeah, and Val. You'll meet 'em. They're the best."

Scarlet couldn't help smiling. She knew those names already. Aunt Jess. Aunt Val. But now... they were just girls. Teenagers.

Missy glanced at her. "You got friends back home?"

Scarlet hesitated. "Yeah. Sort of."

Missy nodded like she got it. "People can be the worst. I swear. Except for, like, your real friends. The ones who show up when you're sick or help you sneak out the window at night."

Scarlet swallowed. "You've done that?"

"Obviously."

Scarlet shook her head with a tiny laugh.

Missy stood up and stretched her arms overhead, squinting at the sky. "You wanna come with me? We're not going anywhere crazy, just down the street. Maybe grab a soda or something."

Scarlet stood too. "Yeah. Okay."

Missy gave her a quick once-over. "You need different shoes if we're walking."

Scarlet looked down at her beat-up sneakers.

Missy smirked. "Don't worry. I got plenty."

And just like that, they were headed inside, Missy already talking about what sneakers would match Scarlet's 'Princeton vibe,' like they'd known each other for years instead of fifteen minutes.

Scarlet followed her, feeling the weirdest mix of nerves and comfort at the same time.

How was she supposed to keep pretending to be someone else... when she was literally standing next to her mom?

Chapter Four

Welcome To Staten Island

Missy's bedroom smelled like Lip Smackers and Aqua Net. A fan hummed lazily in the window, barely moving the heavy summer air. Clothes were everywhere—on the bed, on the dresser, draped over the chair—but somehow, the chaos suited her.

Missy flung open her closet doors and crouched down to dig through a pile of sneakers. "You're lucky I got small feet," she muttered, half to herself.

Scarlet hovered awkwardly by the dresser. She caught sight of a row of framed photos: Missy with friends at some block party, laughing with her head thrown back; another one with a guy in a Yankees jersey who looked like he'd just rolled out of a Spin Doctors video.

Scarlet swallowed hard. This was real. Not just stories or photo albums. This was her mom's life—alive, happening, messy, loud.

Missy sat back on her heels and held up a pair of white platform sneakers with pastel stitching. "What about these? They're, like, totally Clueless-style."

Scarlet smiled despite herself. "Perfect."

Missy tossed them over. "They'll go with your whole... I-don't-know-where-I-am vibe."

Scarlet sat on the edge of the bed to pull them on. They were slightly too big, but manageable.

"Okay," Missy said, standing and fluffing her hair in the mirror. "Now you officially don't look like you got lost at the wrong bus stop."

Scarlet glanced at her. "Thanks. Seriously."

Missy shrugged like it was no big deal. "Like I said—I'm a good judge of character. Plus, it's summer. What else am I gonna do, chores?"

She led the way down the creaky stairs, skipping the last two like she'd done it a thousand times before, and pushed open the front door.

The heat hit them like a blanket. The whole block shimmered with that end-of-August feeling—when summer break felt more like a countdown than a celebration.

They headed down the cracked sidewalk, dodging weeds that pushed up between the concrete squares. Across the street, a group of younger kids were playing wiffle ball, their plastic bat cracked and white with use. Someone's dad washed a car with a hose, water pooling in the gutter.

It all felt like stepping into an old home movie—but one Scarlet somehow knew by heart.

Missy shaded her eyes with her hand. "I was gonna meet up with Jess and Val, but they can wait. Let's grab a soda first."

Scarlet tried to keep her breathing steady. This was really happening. She was walking down the street with her teenage mom.

"Where are we going?" she asked.

"Corner store," Missy said. "It's not 7-Eleven, but they got better candy. You ever have Now and Laters?"

Scarlet blinked. "Yeah... I think so."

Missy laughed. "You're about to get educated."

They turned a corner, and Scarlet felt her heart thump hard against her ribs. Everything was so 1996. The torn concert flyers taped to a telephone pole. A couple of older kids rode past on bikes with handlebars way too high.

It was like walking through one of her mom's old stories—but now she was inside it.

Missy shoved her hands into the back pockets of her cutoffs. "So what's your deal, Carli? You got, like, a boyfriend back in Princeton or what?"

Scarlet almost tripped. "Uh. No. Not really."

Missy gave her a sideways look. "Not really? What's that mean?"

Scarlet searched for an answer that wouldn't break time itself. "It's complicated."

Missy nodded like she totally got it. "They usually are."

They reached the little corner store, the door propped open with a brick. Inside, it was blissfully cool, the hum of the refrigerator cases filling the space.

Missy headed straight for the candy aisle. "I hope you like sour stuff."

Scarlet followed, feeling like she was in some kind of dream. Except the colors were sharper, the sounds clearer, and the girl next to her was about to change her entire life—and didn't even know it yet.

Chapter Five

Corner Store

The little bell over the store door jingled violently as two girls burst inside, loud and full of energy like they owned the whole street.

"Missy!" one of them practically yelled, arms thrown out like she was greeting a long-lost celebrity. "Where the hell have you been?"

Scarlet flinched at the volume, stepping back near the gum rack.

Missy didn't miss a beat. "Relax, Jess. I got distracted."

Jess was tall, lanky, with messy curls piled on her head in a clip, wearing black eyeliner that made her blue eyes pop. She had a wide mouth made for trouble and looked like she was always ready to get into it.

Behind her was Val—shorter, curvier, arms crossed, chewing gum with enough attitude to start a fight with it. Dark brown hair, hoop earrings, and an expression that said she didn't take crap from anybody.

Both girls zeroed in on Scarlet immediately.

Jess narrowed her eyes. "Who's this?"

Missy tossed a candy bar into her basket. "This is Carli. She's from Jersey."

Val raised one eyebrow. "Since when do we hang out with Jersey?"

Missy gave them both a sharp look. "Since now. She's cool."

Scarlet's throat felt dry. She was used to awkward introductions, but this was another level—like getting hazed into a club she didn't sign up for.

Jess smirked. "You got an Jersey accent?"

Scarlet flushed. "I—guess so."

Missy rolled her eyes. "Cool it. She's with me."

That seemed to be enough for Jess, who immediately grabbed a sleeve of powdered donuts off the shelf. "You coming to the beach or what?"

Missy glanced at Scarlet, then back at the girls. "Yeah. Thought I'd bring Carli along."

Val made a face like she wasn't sold yet, but shrugged. "Fine. Hope the guys are there."

Missy shot Scarlet a wink. "They're harmless."

Scarlet wasn't sure she believed that, but something about Missy's confidence made her want to trust it anyway.

Jess leaned over the counter to talk to the bored-looking teenage clerk, already flirting. Val grabbed a Snapple and slapped a crumpled dollar on the counter.

Missy nudged Scarlet with her elbow. "Ready to meet some Farrell boys?"

Scarlet blinked. "Farrell?"

"Archbishop Farrell. Boys' school," Missy explained like it was obvious. "They're usually idiots, but they're hot idiots."

Scarlet let out a nervous laugh. "Great."

Missy grinned like she could already tell how this day was gonna go.

And just like that, Scarlet found herself swept into her mom's world—messy, loud, chaotic, and completely alive.

Chapter Six

The Bikini Drawer

Back at Missy's house, the upstairs hallway was filled with the sound of drawers slamming and hangers clattering. Scarlet sat nervously on the edge of Missy's bed, legs crossed at the ankles, as Missy flung one drawer open after another like she was on a mission from God.

"You're pale," Missy declared, holding a turquoise string bikini up to the light. "But in a classy, expensive way. Like one of those girls in a Ralph Lauren ad."

Scarlet flushed. "Thanks... I think?"

Missy tossed the turquoise bikini aside and pulled out another one—neon pink with black piping. "This one says fun, but also says look at me." She paused, tilting her head.

"You don't seem like a look-at-me kind of girl, though." Scarlet gave a small smile. "Not really."

Missy smirked. "That's okay. You'll get there."

She tossed the pink one onto a growing pile on the bed. "What kind of vibe are you going for? Like girl-next-door? Mysterious stranger from Jersey?"

Scarlet laughed, surprising even herself. "Honestly? One that doesn't fall off if I sneeze."

Missy grinned. "You're funny. Quiet, but funny."

Scarlet looked down at her hands. "I'm just not used to... all this."

Missy turned, one hand on her hip. "All what?"

"This," Scarlet said, motioning vaguely around the room. "Friends who've just met me but take me in like it's no big deal. Beach days with boys. Being in someone else's life."

Missy's expression softened. "Well... now it's your life too. Even if just for today."

Scarlet nodded slowly. There was something about the way Missy said it—so certain, so sure of herself—that made it hard not to believe her.

Missy held up a white bikini with tiny navy flowers. "This one's cute. Not too much, not too boring. It's what I wear when I want people to think I'm innocent."

Scarlet raised an eyebrow. "Are you?"

Missy winked. "Depends who's asking."

She tossed it to Scarlet. "Try it. My bathroom's down the hall. Holler if you get stuck."

Scarlet stood slowly, bikini clutched in her hand like it was something delicate. She paused at the door. "Missy?"

"Yeah?"

Scarlet looked back at her. "Thanks. For... everything."

Missy shrugged, casual. "Whatever. I'm just bored and you're weird. It works."

But there was a smile tugging at the corner of her mouth as she turned back to the drawer, already fishing out her own beach outfit.

In the bathroom, Scarlet stood in front of the mirror for a long moment, the bikini dangling from her fingers. Her reflection stared back—nervous, awkward, pale in the harsh light— but underneath all that, something else was beginning to stir.

A maybe.

A spark.

She tried the bikini on carefully. It didn't fit perfectly, but it wasn't terrible either. She tied the strings, adjusted the top, smoothed the bottom, and finally opened the bathroom door.

Missy looked up from where she was lining her lips in front of the dresser mirror.

She let out a low whistle. "Okay, Carli from Princeton. Look at you."

Scarlet blushed, but smiled anyway. "It's fine, right? Not too much?"

Missy gave her a once-over. "It's perfect. Just enough to make the Farrell boys lose their minds, but not enough to get you in trouble."

Scarlet laughed. She kind of loved that balance.

Missy grabbed her tote bag, stuffed it with magazines, body spray, and a towel, then tossed one to Scarlet. "Let's go. Jess and Val'll be waiting at the bus stop."

Scarlet wrapped the towel around her waist and followed Missy out the door, heart fluttering.

Maybe she wasn't a "look-at-me" kind of girl...yet.

But for today?

She could fake it. She was Carli.

Chapter Seven

The Bus Ride

The bus wheezed as it pulled up to the corner, its doors opening with a hiss. The driver looked like he'd been doing this route since the dawn of time—he didn't even blink at the four girls piling on in oversized sunglasses and beach towels.

Missy dropped a couple of crumpled dollar bills into the fare box, then turned and tugged

Scarlet down the aisle. "Back seat. Always."

The bus smelled like heat, old vinyl, and the faint tang of body spray. A radio someone had rigged near the front was playing "Where Do You Go" by No Mercy, loud enough to make the windows rattle.

Jess was already in the back, smacking her gum and flipping through a *YM* magazine. Val sat beside her with one leg propped up on the seat, sunglasses perched on her head, eating red licorice from a bag like she hadn't eaten in days.

"Look who finally decided to show," Jess said, not looking up.

"Had to get Carli beach-ready," Missy said, sliding into the seat next to her.

Scarlet hesitated, then sat down next to Val, clutching her tote bag like a lifeline.

Val gave her a sideways look. "Cute bikini. Good pick."

Scarlet smiled nervously. "Thanks."

Missy leaned forward between the seats. "Carli's never been to the Staten Island beaches.

We're about to blow her mind."

Jess laughed. "Oh yeah, girl. You're about to see a lot of bad tattoos and guys with their socks still on."

"And don't forget the cologne," Val added, wrinkling her nose. "Like a whole *cloud* of

Drakkar Noir and desperation."

Scarlet grinned, starting to relax. They were wild, loud, and a little terrifying—but in a way that made her feel safer somehow. Like nothing bad could happen while they were around.

Missy twisted around in her seat, tossing her long hair over her shoulder. "Okay. Roll call. Do we have: snacks, lip gloss, radio, emergency quarters, and at least one story we can lie about if we meet hot guys?"

"Check, check, check," Jess said, waving her Snapple.

"Lying is my love language," Val added.

Scarlet bit back a laugh. She was quiet, sure—but not invisible. Not with this crew.

As the bus rumbled past blocks of brick houses and faded corner stores, Missy pulled a small can of body spray from her bag and misted the air in front of them with something vaguely coconut-scented.

Jess coughed. "Jesus, Missy. Trying to choke us?"

"It's called setting the tone," Missy said. "It's beach day."

The bus hit a bump and everyone bounced in their seats. Carli clutched the pole, knuckles white.

"You good?" Val asked, noticing.

"Yeah," Scarlet said. "Just not used to this kind of bus."

Val raised an eyebrow. "What kind of bus do you ride in Princeton? One made of gold?"

Missy leaned over and patted Scarlet's knee. "She's classy. We're corrupting her."

Scarlet looked out the window, watching as the streets changed—more flip-flops, more bikes, more beach chairs being dragged by little kids and their older brothers. The air had that lazy buzz of summer almost over, but not quite.

She let out a breath.

She wasn't just tagging along anymore.

She was part of this now.

Chapter Eight

The Beach

The bus hissed to a stop at the edge of the beach parking lot, its brakes squealing like they were complaining about the heat. The doors swung open, and a wave of hot, salty air rushed in—thick with sunscreen, fried food, and the distant echo of someone's boom box blasting No Doubt.

Missy was the first off the bus, beach tote slung over her shoulder like she was arriving at a red carpet event. Jess and Val followed, both adjusting their sunglasses and talking at the same time. Scarlet stepped down last, blinking against the brightness.

The sand looked like it went on forever—packed with umbrellas, towels, coolers, and Staten Islanders in every shape, shade, and style. Kids darted around half-buried in the sand. Someone had brought a full grill. A dad nearby was already yelling at his son to "get outta the damn water if you can't swim!"

Scarlet stood still for a moment, taking it all in. It wasn't glamorous. It wasn't perfect. But it was alive. Real.

Missy glanced back. "You good?"

Scarlet nodded slowly. "Yeah. Just... wow."

"Welcome to Midland Beach," Missy said, tugging her towel loose and tying it around her waist like a runway model. "Now let's find a good spot before the bridge-and-tunnel crowd invades."

They staked out a spot near the lifeguard chair and unrolled their towels. Jess immediately pulled out tanning oil. Val flopped down and started digging around in her bag for snacks.

Scarlet set her things down slowly, unsure of the rhythm here. She wrapped her towel around herself a little tighter.

Missy clocked it. "You look fine, Carli. Trust me."

Scarlet gave her a grateful half-smile. "I'm trying not to overthink it."

Jess leaned over from her towel. "Rule one of beach day? Don't overthink it. Rule two?

Reapply lip gloss every hour."

"Rule three," Val added, "don't fall for the first Farrell guy you see. They peak at sixteen."

Just as she said it, a small group of guys in mesh shorts and backwards hats strolled across the sand, one of them holding a radio over his shoulder like it was still 1992.

Missy squinted. "Oh my God. Is that Anthony?"

Jess sat up. "Don't even. If that's him, you're gonna make us stalk them all afternoon."

Val sighed dramatically. "Not again."

Scarlet followed their gaze, eyes landing on the tallest guy in the group. Dark hair, Yankees cap, white tee stretched across his shoulders, laughing as he walked. He was definitely cute. And definitely confident.

"Who's Anthony?" Scarlet asked carefully.

Missy didn't answer right away. She kept watching the group, something soft flickering in her eyes. "No one. Just this guy."

Jess muttered, "Just this guy she's written his name on her notebook like a thousand times." Scarlet smiled to herself. So that was the guy.

The Farrell boys passed a few feet away. One of them glanced over—Scarlet couldn't tell which—and nudged the one next to him. They all looked for half a second too long.

Missy, completely unbothered, flipped her hair and reapplied her gloss like it was a performance.

Jess waved. "That one just looked at you, Carli."

Scarlet froze. "What? No he didn't."

"Yeah he did," Val said. "He did the whole up-down thing. You're in."

Scarlet's cheeks burned. "No. I'm not."

Missy gave her a sly smile. "You are now."

Scarlet sat down quickly on her towel, heart racing, pretending to dig through her bag for something she didn't need. She wasn't used to this kind of attention.

But a tiny part of her—the part that was tired of always being the quiet girl, the careful one—didn't hate it.

Chapter Nine

Boys

The sun was high and relentless, beating down on them like it had something to prove. Sunscreen mixed with coconut oil clung to the air, and Scarlet could feel the sweat beading on the back of her neck as she sat cross-legged on her towel, watching Jess and Val bicker over which Spice Girl they were most like.

"I'm obviously Sporty," Val said, flexing her arm. "I literally punched a girl at school for cutting the lunch line."

"You're not Sporty," Jess snapped. "You're Scary. You scare everyone. I'm Sporty."

Missy looked up from her Seventeen magazine. "Jess, you don't even do sports."

"I could if I wanted to," Jess said, and Val tossed a piece of licorice at her.

Scarlet laughed under her breath.

"You can be Baby Spice," Missy said, nodding at Scarlet. "She's quiet but sneaky. The ones like that always get you when you least expect it."

Scarlet raised an eyebrow. "You really think I'm sneaky?"

Missy smirked. "I think you've got layers."

Scarlet didn't know what to say to that. No one had ever told her she had layers before— especially not someone like Missy, who made everything sound like a compliment and a dare at the same time.

A whistle blew from the lifeguard chair, snapping them out of it.

Jess rolled over. "Ugh. I can't even relax without someone drowning."

Val leaned on one elbow and jerked her chin toward the group of Farrell boys now posted up a few towels down. "They've been looking over here every five seconds. Bet they're working up the nerve."

Missy didn't even glance. "They better. I didn't shave my legs for nothing."

Scarlet snorted, then clapped a hand over her mouth, shocked she'd let that slip.

Missy turned and grinned. "See? Told you. You're low-key hilarious."

"Low-key hilarious," Jess echoed in a sing-song voice. "That's the best kind."

Scarlet felt the warmth in her cheeks, but this time it wasn't just embarrassment. It was something else—something good. These girls weren't teasing her to be mean. They were letting her in.

Missy stood and shook out her towel dramatically. "Okay. I'm going in."

"In that water?" Jess made a face. "You're braver than me."

Missy pointed at her. "That's 'cause I'm Sporty Spice."

Val groaned. "God help us."

Missy turned to Scarlet. "You coming?"

Scarlet hesitated, eyes flicking to the Farrell boys again. One of them was definitely watching her—maybe the same one from earlier.

She looked up at Missy.

"Yes," she said, standing. "I'm coming."

They walked toward the water together, towels around their waists, sun blazing down on their shoulders. The sand burned Scarlet's feet, but she didn't care. She was walking next to the coolest girl she'd ever met, wearing a borrowed bikini from the 90s, and someone cute was maybe looking at her.

Missy glanced sideways. "Just so you know... if one of those guys tries to talk to you, don't freeze up."

Scarlet laughed. "I probably will."

"Don't," Missy said. "Just smile and look like you have a secret."

Scarlet tilted her head. "What kind of secret?"

Missy shrugged. "Doesn't matter. Boys are dumb. If they think you know something they don't, they'll follow you around all day trying to figure it out."

Scarlet smiled to herself as they reached the edge of the water. The waves rolled in warm and choppy, splashing against their ankles.

She felt like she was standing on the edge of something bigger than just the ocean.

And for once, she wasn't afraid to take the next step. Or at least Carli wasn't.

Chapter Ten

Girl Talk

The sun was lower now, casting everything in that hazy gold that made even Staten Island look like a movie. Missy flopped back on her towel, hair damp and sea-salted, sunglasses slipping down her nose.

Scarlet sat cross-legged next to her, towel wrapped tightly around her shoulders. Her skin was warm, a little pink, but not burnt. Progress.

Jess had moved on to braiding a long strand of seaweed into Val's hair while Val threatened to knock her teeth out every few seconds.

"You do it again, I swear—"

"Relax," Jess said. "It's a beach accessory."

Val swatted at her. "You're gonna be a missing person accessory."

Missy laughed, then turned her head toward Carli. "So what's your deal, really?"

Scarlet blinked. "What do you mean?"

"I mean..." Missy propped herself up on one elbow, "You show up at my house like you fell out of the sky. You're super polite. You talk like you read books for fun. And you've got this whole... mystery vibe."

Scarlet shifted a little. "I told you—I hit my head. Things are just fuzzy."

Missy didn't press. She just nodded like she got it. "Yeah. Life's fuzzy sometimes."

There was a pause, quiet except for the distant sound of a boom box blasting Tupac from down the beach.

Then Scarlet asked, "Do you ever think about the future?"

Missy raised an eyebrow. "Like college and jobs and all that?"

Scarlet nodded.

Missy flopped back on the towel again. "Sometimes. But mostly I think about getting through the next week without my mom losing her mind about my room."

Scarlet smiled. "She seems... strict."

"She is," Missy said. "But she's also, like, obsessed with pretending everything's perfect. Church every Sunday. Napkins folded like we're having the Pope over. Meanwhile, my dad's barely home, always working and my brothers are always getting into fights."

Scarlet turned her face toward her. "You don't talk about that much, do you?"

Missy paused. "Not really. Doesn't matter. I'm gonna get out of here someday. Open my own salon. Do hair. Not just my friends and cousins."

Scarlet's eyes lit up. "That's awesome. You'd be really good at that."

Missy glanced at her. "You think so?"

Scarlet nodded, completely sincere. "You've got a way of making people feel... seen. I think you'd be amazing."

For a second, Missy didn't say anything. Then she looked away, like she didn't want Carli to see her smile.

"Thanks," she said, voice a little quieter.

Scarlet leaned back on her elbows, watching the clouds drift across the sky.

For the first time since she arrived, she felt like she belonged here, being Carli—not because she was trying to fit in, but because these girls were letting her be exactly who she was.

The quiet one. The listener. The one with layers.

Missy threw a handful of sand into the air. "Next time, we bring more chips. And no more seaweed, Jess, I'm serious."

"Ugh, fine," Jess groaned.

"Also," Val added, eyes closed, "next time, we do Ralph's Ices after. I need lemon cherry like I need air."

Scarlet smiled to herself. These girls were wild, chaotic, ridiculous—and she adored them already.

She had no idea how long she'd be stuck here.

Chapter Eleven

7-11

The bus ride back felt slower, sleepier. Everyone had that end-of-beach-day glow—tanned legs stretched out, flip-flops dangling from fingers, towels slung lazily over shoulders.

Jess had fallen asleep with her mouth wide open, her head bouncing slightly against the window every time the bus hit a pothole. Val was chewing on the last of her red licorice, sunglasses still on even though the sun had dipped behind the buildings.

Scarlet sat quietly, pressed up against the window, watching the houses blur past—chainlink fences, crooked porches, rusted basketball hoops. She didn't say much, but her mind was full. Of Farrell boys. Of Missy. Of how strange and perfect this day had been.

Missy nudged her. "You good?"

Scarlet nodded. "Yeah. Just tired."

Missy yawned and leaned her head back. "Same. Sun takes it outta you. So does babysitting Jess and Val."

Val flipped her off without looking.

The bus slowed. "This is us," Missy said, standing and tugging Carli's wrist. "C'mon. Jess, Val—see you tomorrow!"

Jess mumbled something unintelligible and waved without opening her eyes.

The girls stepped off the bus into the thick, golden hour heat. It was quieter now, the sidewalks mostly empty except for a few dads pulling out garbage cans and some kids tossing a football in the street.

Missy turned to Scarlet. "Wanna stop at 7-Eleven?"

Scarlet hesitated. "Yeah. Sure."

It was only a block away, buzzing fluorescent lights flickering above the door, the air inside deliciously cold as they stepped in.

Missy made a beeline for the Slurpee machine. "Blue raspberry or cherry?"

Scarlet glanced at the machine. "Can I mix them?"

Missy grinned. "Now you're catching on."

They filled their cups, grabbed a bag of chips and a couple of candy bars, and collapsed onto the curb out front, plastic bags rustling between them.

Scarlet took a long sip of her Slurpee. Her head buzzed from the cold, but it felt good.

Missy unwrapped a candy bar. "So, real talk. That beach was a lot. You okay?"

Scarlet nodded. "Yeah. I think so."

"You looked a little... I dunno. Shell-shocked."

Scarlet shrugged. "I'm just not used to that much attention. Or people. Or... fun, honestly."

Missy looked over, her face softening. "What's life like back home?"

Scarlet paused. "Quiet. I have friends, but we're not like you guys. Everything's kind of... safe. Predictable."

Missy took another bite, chewing thoughtfully. "That sounds kinda nice."

Scarlet looked at her. "You think?"

"Yeah," Missy said. "My life's never predictable. Sometimes I wish it was."

They sat in silence for a minute, sipping their Slurpees as the sky turned orange and purple above them.

Then Missy asked, "You wanna crash at my place tonight? Jess and Val'll get over it."

Scarlet blinked. "Really?"

"Yeah. Why not? I got the good hair stuff, and I just taped Clueless off HBO. You ever seen it?"

Scarlet smiled. "Once. A long time ago."

Missy stood and offered her a hand. "Well you're due for a rewatch."

Scarlet took it, standing slowly.

Maybe she'd wake up tomorrow and this would all be gone.

But for tonight, under the glow of a 7-Eleven sign, it felt real.

It felt like the beginning of something.

Chapter Twelve

Clueless & Clues

Missy's bedroom was lit only by the soft glow of a lava lamp and the flickering blue of the TV screen. The VHS tape was slightly fuzzy—recorded off HBO, like she'd said—but Clueless still looked perfect. Alicia Silverstone leaned over her white Jeep, whining about her report card.

"Ugh, I love her," Missy said, lying on her stomach, chin in her hands. "She's like... annoying but perfect."

Scarlet sat cross-legged on the floor, a towel draped over her shoulders, her wet hair wrapped in a T-shirt. "She's really confident."

Missy nodded. "Yeah. And she talks like she knows what she wants. I respect that."

She reached over and dabbed a glob of deep conditioner into her palm, then started raking it through her hair like a pro.

Scarlet stared at her reflection in the mirror across the room. Her face looked softer in the low light. Less tense. Like maybe she was starting to fit in. Being Carli had its moments.

Missy turned to her. "Wanna do yours?"

Scarlet blinked. "My hair?"

"Yeah. It's good hair, Carli. Just needs some Staten Island TLC."

Scarlet laughed and moved over to sit in front of her. Missy started working the product through her damp hair, fast but careful.

"You're really good at this," Scarlet said.

Missy shrugged. "I've been doing hair since I was like eight. Cousins, aunts, my mom when she lets me."

Scarlet was quiet a second, then said, "You're gonna be really good at it someday."

Missy paused mid-section. "You really think that?"

Scarlet looked up at her. "I know it."

Missy smiled, then kept working in silence for a while. On the TV, Cher and Dionne argued about fashion rules while Scarlet's hair slowly turned into something softer, shinier, almost floaty.

They settled back onto the bed, towels wrapped around their shoulders, sipping warm Diet Cokes from cans Missy had smuggled up earlier.

'I just love this movie. It's gonna be a classic."

Scarlet smiled, playing along. "Yeah, it's really good. Cher's wardrobe is next-level."

Missy grinned. "You can never see Clueless too many times."

Then Scarlet asked, "So what are you doing after high school?"

Missy tilted her head. "Beauty school, probably. Unless I marry someone rich, which— honestly? Not a great plan, given my taste in guys."

Scarlet smiled.

Missy leaned back against the pillows, chewing her lip. "Everyone acts like you're supposed to know what comes next. But how? I don't even know what I'm doing next week."

Scarlet nodded slowly. "It's scary."

"Yeah." Missy looked over. "What about you? What do you wanna do?"

Scarlet hesitated. "I think... I want to be someone who's not afraid to try things. To speak up. To take chances. Even if it's messy."

Missy stared at her for a second. "That's deep."

Scarlet smirked. "Sorry."

"No," Missy said quickly. "I like it."

They sat in silence for a while, letting the movie play, the lava lamp casting soft blobs of red and blue on the ceiling.

Then Missy suddenly gasped. "Oh my God. We should see Titanic when it comes out."

Scarlet almost choked on her soda.

Missy narrowed her eyes. "What?"

Scarlet recovered quickly. "Nothing. I just heard it's, um... gonna be huge."

"You think?" Missy flopped onto her back. "Ugh, I love Leonardo DiCaprio. I saw him in that Romeo movie and, like... I would die for him."

Scarlet giggled into her sleeve. "You're not alone."

They stayed like that for a while—half watching the movie, half drifting into that sleepy, sun-warmed silence only summer nights can give you.

Scarlet didn't know how long this would last. How much time she had. But right now, wrapped in a towel with glossy hair and a full heart, she felt okay.

Maybe better than okay.

Chapter Thirteen

Mall Madness

The next day they decided to do a mall trip.

The Staten Island Mall was packed—blasting air conditioning, sticky tile floors, and a cloud of perfume hovering near the entrance of Macy's. Every teenage girl in the borough seemed to be there, all walking in packs, carrying Wet Seal bags and giggling like it was an Olympic sport.

"First stop: Wet Seal," Missy declared, leading the charge like a general with a mission. "I need something to wear for the block party."

Scarlet followed, flanked by Jess and Val, trying to take it all in. The fluorescent lights, the jangly mall music, the way the food court always kind of smelled like pretzels and cleaning fluid—it was overwhelming in the best way.

Jess walked backward for a few steps, pointing her straw at Missy. "You already have fifty outfits."

Missy didn't miss a beat. "And not one that says fun but untouchable."

"You're so dramatic," Val muttered, sipping her Orange Julius.

Inside Wet Seal, the racks were full of spaghetti strap dresses, platform sandals, and glittery halter tops. Carli wandered toward a rack of butterfly clips, touching one like it was made of glass.

Missy noticed. "You like those?"

Scarlet nodded. "I had some... I mean, I saw some before."

Missy plucked one off the display and clipped it gently into Carli's hair. "There. Now you officially belong."

Scarlet smiled, tucking her hair behind her ear. "Thanks."

Val held up a tiny black mini-skirt. "Okay but *this* with a chunky heel and a choker? Forget it."

Jess snorted. "Yeah, if you're trying to get expelled."

"From what?" Val said. "We're not even in school yet."

Missy held up a shimmery silver top to her chest and stared at herself in the mirror. "This says *I don't care if you like me* while secretly hoping he does."

"Speaking of *he*...." Jess said suddenly, eyes narrowing.

Scarlet turned.

Walking past the store—flanked by two other Farrell boys—was Anthony.

Dark hair. Clean white t-shirt. Gold chain. That same confident swagger from the beach, like he didn't even realize people were watching. Or maybe he *did*.

Missy went still.

Jess muttered, "Of *course* he's here."

Val sucked her teeth. "He's probably here for cologne. He always smells like he rolled in *Cool Water*."

Scarlet tried to read Missy's face. But it was unreadable. Calm. Blank. Too blank.

Anthony hadn't seen them—yet. He passed by the storefront without glancing in. Missy turned slowly, watching his back.

Jess raised an eyebrow. "Say something."

Missy flipped the silver top back onto the rack. "Nope."

Val scoffed. "Why not?"

"Because," Missy said, suddenly busy with her purse. "He's not worth chasing."

Scarlet watched her closely. The way she faked coolness so fast. The way her hands trembled just a little as she zipped her bag.

Missy turned to them. "I'm starving. Food court?"

Jess and Val both said "Yes" in unison, already walking.

Scarlet hesitated beside Missy. "Are you okay?"

Missy didn't look at her. "Totally."

But as they walked, Scarlet noticed Missy glancing back once—just once—toward the hallway where Anthony had disappeared.

Chapter Fourteen

Write It On A T-Shirt

The Sbarro counter was a wall of glowing orange heat lamps and greasy deliciousness. Jess ordered first—two slices of pepperoni and a Sprite—while Val claimed a red booth near the fountain soda station like she was planting a flag.

Missy and Scarlet trailed behind, each carrying a tray with a slice, a soda, and a side of mall weariness.

Missy dropped into the booth beside Val, already pulling napkins out like a magician. Scarlet sat across from them, the Formica table sticky under her arms.

Jess flopped into the remaining seat and unwrapped her straw with her teeth. "I swear, mall food slaps harder in the summer."

Val held up her slice like a toast. "To carbs and crushes."

Missy snorted, but didn't say anything. She was pulling at the edge of her straw wrapper like it owed her money.

Scarlet took a careful bite of her pizza and glanced across the table. "So... who is Anthony, exactly?"

Val and Jess answered at the same time.

"Trouble," Jess said.

"Missy's bad idea in a Yankees cap," Val added, deadpan.

Missy rolled her eyes. "You two are so dramatic."

Scarlet gave her a gentle look. "You like him, though."

Missy shrugged, chewing. "We talked. A couple times. Nothing serious."

"But you want it to be," Carli said softly.

Missy paused, then took a long sip of her soda. "Yeah. I guess I do."

Jess leaned forward. "He's not the worst, but he's got a reputation. He's hot, and he knows it. That combo never ends well."

Val nodded. "He was seeing that girl from Holy Child—what's her name?"

"Gabby," Missy said under her breath.

"Right. Gabby," Val snapped her gum. "Big hair, big mouth, bigger attitude. You could take her, though."

Scarlet tilted her head. "You think he's still seeing her?"

Missy looked down at her tray. "I don't know."

The table quieted for a minute, save for the sound of chewing and the dull hum of 'Kiss Me' by Sixpence None the Richer playing somewhere in the background.

Scarlet sipped her soda slowly. "Can I ask you something?"

Missy looked up. "Always."

"What would you do... if you had one summer that might change everything?"

Missy blinked. "Like... this one?"

Scarlet nodded.

Missy leaned back. "I guess I'd make it count. Wear the outfit. Kiss the guy. Laugh too loud.

Stay up too late."

Jess grinned. "Write that on a T-shirt."

Scarlet smiled to herself. Maybe she'd do all of that. Or maybe she'd just stay here as long as she could—soaking it all in before the real world came calling.

Val pushed her tray away and stood. "C'mon. I want to go try on lip liner I'm not gonna buy."

Missy stood too, grabbing her bag. "We're hitting Contempo Casuals next."

Jess groaned. "I'm gonna need another soda for that."

They shuffled away from the booth, leaving crumbs, empty cups, and a trail of inside jokes behind them.

Scarlet lingered for a moment, trailing her fingers along the edge of the red plastic cup.

This summer was borrowed.

But for now, it was hers.

Chapter Fifteen

Truth Or Dare

Back at Missy's house, the sun had dipped lower, casting a warm, sleepy glow across the porch. The screen door squeaked as the girls filed in, dropping their bags in a heap near the stairs.

Missy's mom poked her head out from the kitchen. "You girls eat?"

"Like animals," Missy called back.

"Good. Dinner's at six. Don't spoil your appetites."

Missy rolled her eyes as they headed upstairs.

"Everything's an appetite spoiler to her. Gum, grapes, life."

Scarlet smiled, trailing behind her into the bedroom. The windows were cracked open, letting in the cicada buzz of late summer. Missy flopped on her bed dramatically, grabbing a remote and flicking on the small TV. Static crackled before an episode of *Friends* came into view.

Jess and Val dropped onto the floor like they owned it. Val already had a bottle of glitter nail polish out, shaking it like a pro. Jess flipped through a teen magazine, stopping every few pages to read a quiz out loud.

"Okay—'Would you rather date a guy who has a pager but never returns your beep, or one who calls your house so much your dad starts answering with threats?'"

"Ugh, neither," Missy groaned. "Next."

Scarlet sat cross-legged by the bed, brushing damp hair off her forehead. She still smelled like mall pizza and Sun-In. She wasn't even mad about it.

Val looked up from her toes. "Hey Carli, truth or dare?"

"Truth," Scarlet said cautiously.

"Who was your first kiss?"

Scarlet hesitated. "This kid in fifth grade. It was during a game of spin the bottle. Super awkward."

The girls howled with laughter.

"Was he cute at least?" Jess asked.

Scarlet shrugged. "Had like a rat tail."

"Oh my God!" Missy cackled. "A rat tail? That's Staten Island romance right there."

The laughter melted into something softer. Familiar. Easy.

Missy turned the volume down on the TV. "Okay, serious moment."

All eyes turned toward her.

"What's something you've never told anyone?"

Val groaned. "I thought this was a hangout, not a therapy session."

They were still laughing when Missy's mom's voice echoed up the stairs:
"Dinner's ready! Move it before your father eats all the bread!"

They all scrambled down the hallway, the scent of garlic bread and red sauce already filling the air.

After dinner, just as the girls were settling into a post-pasta haze, a distant jingle echoed down the block.

"The ice cream truck!" Missy shouted, already halfway to the door.

The girls tumbled out of the house barefoot, chasing the music with dollar bills in their hands and laughter trailing behind them.

Chapter Sixteen

Sunday Sauce

Sunday morning started with the smell of coffee and Aqua Net.

Missy's house was buzzing before 9 a.m.—drawers opening, blow dryers blasting, someone yelling down the hall about a missing belt. Carli stood in the bathroom brushing her hair, still in borrowed clothes, still stunned that somehow... this had become normal.

Missy walked by the door in a floral sundress and kitten heels, teasing her bangs with one hand and holding a can of Rave hairspray in the other.

"You better hustle," she said, peeking into the mirror beside her. "We do not make my mother late for church. She'll literally pray for your soul right there in the pew."

Scarlet scrambled to finish getting ready—Missy had thrown together an outfit for her: a knee-length floral skirt, a cardigan with pearly buttons, and kitten heels that felt like they belonged to someone braver. Her hair was freshly brushed, clipped with one of Missy's butterfly clips, and her nerves were buzzing under her skin.

The church was five blocks away, and they walked there in a line—Missy, Scarlet, Missy's younger brothers elbowing each other the whole time, and her parents trailing behind with that familiar half-fighting, half-flirting energy that only long-married couples had.

Inside, it was all cool air, stained glass, and incense. Old ladies clutched their rosaries like lifelines. Teen boys slouched in pews like they were serving time. The priest's voice droned from the altar like a fog rolling through marble.

Missy slid into a pew, kneeling and crossing herself so fast it looked like muscle memory. Carli followed awkwardly, mimicking the motions. She hadn't been to a church like this in years.

Missy leaned over. "Don't fall asleep during the homily. My mom will know."

Scarlet smiled. "Noted."

The music started—soft organ notes rising into the rafters. Scarlet sat back, taking it in. The light streaming through the windows. The kneelers creaking. The quiet rhythm of people rising, sitting, kneeling again like it was choreographed.

There was a kind of comfort in it. Not her world—but she understood it.

After communion, Missy whispered, "One more hymn, then it's sauce and insanity."

Scarlet raised an eyebrow. "What?"

"Sunday dinner," Missy said with a wink. "We eat like we're feeding the entire island. You'll see."

Back at the house, the air was thick with garlic, basil, and simmering tomato sauce. Sinatra played from a dusty stereo. Missy's mom was at the stove with an apron tied over her dress, shouting instructions in Italian-English to no one in particular.

The table was already set for at least twelve. Scarlet couldn't tell who was actually family and who was just invited—but everyone was loud, affectionate, and already halfway into a debate about the Yankees' chances this year.

"Wetteland's lights out," one uncle said, waving a fork.

"Yeah, but Rivera's the real weapon," another added.

"They better not blow it in October," someone muttered through a mouthful of bread.

Missy pulled Scarlet into the kitchen and handed her a spoon. "Stir the sauce. But don't let it bubble over or my mother will have you excommunicated."

Scarlet laughed, then actually stirred—slow, careful, soaking in the moment.

Missy's dad walked in, kissed his wife on the cheek, and stole a meatball right out of the pot. She smacked his hand and called him *disgrazia*, but she was smiling.

It was chaos. It was love. It was home.

And for Scarlet, it was all a little overwhelming.

They finally sat to eat—huge bowls of pasta, baskets of crusty bread, plates of sliced sausage and peppers, salad that no one touched. Wine for the grown-ups, soda in red plastic cups for the kids.

Scarlet sat beside Missy, answering questions about "where she's from" and nodding along like she wasn't from *the future*. No one seemed to notice. Or maybe they just didn't care. She belonged here today, and that was enough.

At one point, Missy's dad raised a glass. "To family," he said. "To keeping it together, even when everything's nuts."

Scarlet caught Missy's eye across the table. Missy smiled, lifted her glass, and clinked it gently against Carli's.

And in that moment, Scarlet felt it—that warm ache in her chest.

She didn't know how long this would last.

But she knew she'd remember it forever.

Chapter Seventeen

Sleepover At Missy's

The night felt electric from the start.

After Sunday dinner, Scarlet thought maybe the day was winding down—but Missy had other plans. "Sleepover time," she announced, already halfway up the stairs. "Go grab your pajama pants and get ready to sing your heart out."

Jess and Val were already there by the time Scarlet changed into borrowed flannel pants and an oversized Bon Jovi tee. Missy's room looked like a scene out of a teen magazine— *YM* or *Seventeen* maybe—with posters of Leonardo DiCaprio, Gavin Rossdale, and the entire cast of *Party of Five* taped to the walls. A lava lamp glowed pink in the corner, and a boom box was blasting the *Spice Girls* on cassette.

"I call Sporty!" Jess shouted, twirling a hairbrush like a microphone.

"I'm obviously Baby," Val said, puckering her lips as she applied a thick coat of bubblegum pink Lip Smackers.

Scarlet hesitated for a second until Missy handed her a glittery clip. "You're Posh. Trust me."

The room erupted into dancing and laughter, socks sliding across the carpet, hairbrush karaoke in full force. They lip-synced to *Say You'll Be There*, then *Wannabe*, collapsing into giggles every time someone forgot a line.

Missy pulled out her Caboodles case and flipped it open dramatically. "Okay, beauty hour.

Who's first?"

Val plopped down in front of her. "Just don't over-tweeze my brows this time."

"You're welcome for last time," Missy said, already working with a pencil-thin precision.

Jess painted Carli's nails a metallic lavender while asking, "So, Carli... do you think you'll stay here? Like, in Staten Island?"

Scarlet hesitated. "I don't know yet."

"Girl of mystery," Jess said, raising an eyebrow. "I like it."

They moved on to hair curlers, butterfly clips, and shimmery eyeshadow. Missy curled Scarlet's hair section by section, misting it with apple-scented hairspray. "This is your makeover montage moment," she said. "Cue the *Clueless* soundtrack."

They laughed until their sides hurt. Someone brought out a bag of sour gummy worms and a 2-liter of Pepsi. Missy's little brother knocked on the door once to complain about the noise, and they screamed in unison for him to "get lost."

Later, with the music turned down low and the lights dimmed, the four of them lay on the floor in sleeping bags, staring at the glow-in-the-dark stars Missy had stuck to her ceiling.

"Do you think we'll remember this night when we're old?" Val asked dreamily.

"I better," Jess muttered. "My hair will never be this perfect again."

Scarlet smiled in the dark. Something inside her felt full—like she'd stepped into a life she didn't know she needed. A part of her longed to stay suspended in that moment forever, where everything felt light and simple and full of magic.

She didn't know what tomorrow would bring. But tonight, she belonged.

Chapter Eighteen

Block Party Begins...

Labor Day morning came with the buzz of excitement thick in the air. Even before noon, Scarlet could hear the sounds of folding tables clattering onto sidewalks, someone's dad dragging out the big speakers, and kids already running through the sprinklers in their bathing suits.

Missy's whole block was transforming before their eyes. Bunting in red, white, and blue hung from porch railings, the smell of sausage and peppers wafted from someone's grill, and every mom on the street had a tray of something wrapped in foil.

Inside, the girls were getting ready like it was prom.

"Okay," Missy said, hands on her hips. "We go big today or we stay home."

Jess was in front of the mirror, curling her hair with a Conair iron while Val layered lip liner like her life depended on it. Missy, of course, looked perfect in a black spaghetti strap dress that hugged her curves, chunky black platform sandals, and a gold nameplate necklace that caught the light every time she moved.

Scarlet stood by the window, watching the block fill with people. "This is really a thing, huh?"

"A Staten Island tradition," Val said. "Like Sunday sauce and overprotective uncles."

By early afternoon, the party was in full swing. Tables lined the block, loaded with trays of baked ziti, meatballs, antipasto, cookies from Royal Crown, and pitchers of lemonade. A boom box blasted Freestyle hits and Gloria Estefan. Kids zoomed around on scooters, and every dad had a cold beer in one hand and a story to tell with the other.

Missy scanned the crowd, trying to act casual. "Do you see him?" she asked, brushing her hair back like it wasn't on purpose.

Jess smirked. "Anthony? Yeah. He's over by the cooler, looking all 'too cool' in that chain and wife-beater tank."

Scarlet followed Missy's gaze. There he was—Anthony. Dark curls, deep tan, and that smirk that could start trouble. Missy smoothed her dress and walked over like it was nothing.

Scarlet and the others stayed back, pretending not to watch while absolutely watching.

Anthony looked up and smiled as Missy approached. "Hey, Miss. You look nice."

Missy shrugged. "Thanks. It's nothing."

"You here with your friends?" he asked, cracking open a soda.

"Yeah. You?"

He laughed. "Nah, I crashed. My cousin lives a few doors down."

They chatted for a few minutes—easy, flirty, the way you talk when summer's almost over and you want to hold onto something sweet.

Scarlet watched from across the street, heart twisting just a little. Not in jealousy—but in awe. Her mother—*Missy*—had once been this girl. Confident. Bold. Dreaming.

And Scarlet wasn't just watching it happen.

She was part of it.

Chapter Nineteen

Heartbreak On Henderson Avenue

As the sun dipped lower behind the houses, the block party only grew louder. The music shifted to something faster—C+C Music Factory followed by a burst of *La Bouche*. Someone had dragged a speaker right onto the pavement, and a makeshift dance floor took shape under the string lights.

Missy was glowing. She spun once in the middle of the crowd, letting her hair fly, her laughter spilling out as she pulled Carli and the girls into the circle.

"You got moves, Carli!" Jess laughed, clapping along.

"I learned from Paula Abdul," Carli shot back, feeling free in a way she hadn't since arriving.

Then Scarlet noticed Anthony again—this time leaning back against a car, arms crossed, watching. Missy caught his eye and smiled. He gave her a little nod. Just when it seemed like he might come over—someone else beat him to it.

A girl.

She was older than Missy. Maybe eighteen, maybe already graduated. Tall, tan, with thick auburn curls and way too much lip liner. She walked right up to Anthony and took his hand, pulling him toward the center of the street.

"Who's *that*?" Jess asked, eyes narrowing.

Val rolled her eyes. "One of the Tottenville girls. They think they're grown."

Missy saw it. Scarlet could tell. Her smile faltered, just slightly. She looked away fast and focused on dancing, but something had shifted.

A few songs later, Missy excused herself to grab a soda. Carli stood with Jess and Val near the dessert table, watching the scene unfold like a slow-motion car crash.

"That girl's been all over him," Val muttered. "Look at her laugh. Like she's the funniest thing alive."

Scarlet felt the knot forming in her stomach.

It wasn't until later, after the sun had fully set and the street was glowing with string lights and citronella candles, that it happened.

Jess came rushing over, a little breathless. "Missy—hey. You need to come with me."

Missy raised an eyebrow. "What's up?"

"Just come."

Scarlet followed behind as Jess led them halfway down the block and pointed subtly. Across the street, behind a neighbor's hedge, Anthony and the redhead were standing too close.

Laughing. Whispering.

And then they kissed.

Not a peck. A real kiss.

Scarlet saw Missy go still. Her shoulders dropped just a bit. She didn't cry, didn't run, didn't scream.

She just stared.

Then turned and walked back toward the party like nothing had happened.

But Scarlet could tell—something inside her had cracked.

Chapter Twenty

When It Was Almost Perfect

The block party was winding down.

Paper plates fluttered across the sidewalk, the scent of barbecue lingering in the humid night air. Kids were being herded toward bedtime, the music had softened, and the street was slowly emptying, like a dream dissolving.

"Alright, I'm out," Val said, tossing her empty soda cup in a trash bag. "My mom's gonna kill me if I don't help clean up tomorrow."

"Me too," Jess yawned. "Call me in the morning, Miss. We'll dissect the damage."

Missy nodded, managing a small smile. "Later, girls."

Scarlet lingered beside her as they waved their friends off. She didn't say anything, not yet.

They walked back toward Missy's house together, feet dragging slightly. The night air was thick with the leftover heat of the day, but it had cooled just enough to be pleasant.

As they approached the front steps, Missy's mom was already sitting there—Mrs. Russo, with a tall iced tea in hand and her reading glasses perched on her head.

"You girls have fun?" she asked gently.

Missy plopped down next to her. "Something like that."

Scarlet stayed quiet, settling a few steps below them, her chin resting on her knees as she watched.

Mrs. Russo gave her daughter a once-over, sensing something beneath the silence. "Wanna tell me what's going on?"

Missy sighed. "Anthony kissed some other girl."

"Oh, sweetheart..." her mom said, wrapping an arm around her. "Boys are dumb. Especially the cute ones. It's a rule."

Missy laughed, even as her eyes glistened. "I thought maybe... I don't know. Doesn't matter."

"It does," her mom said softly. "It always matters. But the right boy won't leave you guessing."

Scarlet's throat tightened. She felt like an outsider and an insider all at once—watching her mother, as a teenager, being comforted by the woman she'd only known as Grandma in family photo albums.

There was something so ordinary and yet extraordinary about it.

The streetlamp cast a warm glow over the three of them, the night settling in like a soft quilt.

Missy leaned her head on her mom's shoulder. "Thanks, Ma."

Mrs. Russo kissed her temple. "Always."

Scarlet didn't speak, but inside, something shifted. It was the first time she realized that maybe, just maybe, love ran deeper than heartache—that the women in her family had always been stronger than they looked.

And maybe she was, too.

Chapter Twenty-One

The Polaroid

The sun streamed through the curtains, soft and golden, signaling the start of another summer day - but everything felt different.

Missy stirred in her bed, groaning as she pulled the pillow over her head. "Do we have to get up?"

Scarlet lay on the floor in a sleeping bag, staring at the ceiling, heart still heavy from the night before. "We probably should."

Missy finally sat up, hair a little wild, mascara faintly smudged under the eyes. "Okay, real talk," she said. "I know we've had fun - like, the most fun - but we need to figure out how to get you home."

Scarlet nodded slowly. " I was thinking the same thing."

Missy looked over at her. "You said you don't remember much about how you got here, right" Maybe there's a clue. A name? A place? Family? Someone should be looking for you?"

Scarlet chewed her lip. "It happened so fast. I remember waking up in your room. I was wearing my own clothes...I had my necklace..." She reached up to touch it instinctively.

Missy stood and stretched. "Let's retrace your steps. Maybe something got left behind. Something that'll help."

Scarlet nodded and stood too.

"Can you grab a hoodie from the closet?" Missy asked, already sifting through a drawer for clues. "Might be chilly later."

Scarlet crossed the room, opened the closet door-

-and everything exploded.

A stack of old board games came tumbling down. A shoebox hit her shoulder. Something heavy-a yearbook? A photo album? - whacked her square on the head.

"Ow!" she yelped, falling backward.

But when she blinked, the room had changed.

The posters were gone. The old TV. The incense. The cassette tapes.

In their place: sleek furniture, a smartphone charger on the desk, a framed photo of her and her mom.

Scarlet sat up, dazed, breath catching in her throat.

She was back.

Melissa's closet. 2025. The sound of a shower running down the hall. A laundry basket in the corner. The same necklace around her neck.

The same heart pounding in her chest.

Had it really happened? Had she really met Missy-her mom-or was it just a dream?

Scarlet looked around, still stunned, still half-expecting Jess and Val to come barreling in with snacks and hair rollers.

But it was quiet.

Just her.

She sat for a bit, just to get her head right. As she was about to get up, she noticed another polaroid on the floor.

She reached for it with careful fingers, as though it might disappear if she touched it too quickly. The picture was slightly faded, the edges curled. It showed a girl on the Staten Island Ferry—wind in her hair, a nervous half-smile frozen in time. Her.

Carli.

She stared at it for a long time, turning it over in her hands like it might give her answers. On the back, in faint blue pen, was a name written in all caps.

CARLI D.

Her breath caught.

She let the Polaroid rest on her knee and reached for a second polaroid beside it.

It was another photo.

Her mom again. Younger. Happier. Standing on the deck of the Staten Island Ferry.

And beside her.... Anthony.

He had his arm draped around her shoulder, both of them grinning like it was the best day of their lives. Written in thick black marker on the bottom:

"Me & Anthony DeLuca – Summer '96"

Scarlet froze. She looked back at the first Polaroid, then at the second. Her chest tightened, not with fear, but with a kind of aching clarity.

DeLuca.

She blinked.

Scarlet DeLuca.

Her whole world shifted in one name.

"DeLuca," she whispered. "Scarlet DeLuca."

She felt the room press in around her, soft and golden and full of secrets. It had all happened. Every minute of it.

There was a sound from the hallway—the familiar creak of the floorboards. Her mom's voice, muffled but close.

"Scarlet? Can you help me with the sauce?"

Scarlet blinked, her throat tight.

And then, with the photo still in her hand, she stood up, walked to the door, and called out— "Mooooooom?!!!!!!!"

About the author

K.S. DeLuca grew up on Staten Island with a deep love for summer block parties, butterfly clips, and stories that blend nostalgia with heart.

She now lives in New Jersey, where she writes books inspired by her roots, her family, and the memories that never quite let go.

When she's not writing, she's likely watching reruns of "Friends," sipping an iced chai, working out and daydreaming about the next story.

Bonus Content

SNEAK PEEK: THE WINTER I MET MY DAD

It was snowing the night Scarlet opened the box. A red velvet ribbon untied easily, almost like it had been waiting for her. Inside were newspaper clippings, a pressed white carnation, and a photograph she didn't recognize. But the name on the back was familiar — too familiar.

She turned to the window, watched the snow fall over Princeton, and knew her story wasn't finished.

This time, the past might have even more secrets to tell...

Bonus Features

Step back into 1996 with our Summer Time Capsule Missy's 1996 Soundtrack

-"Wannabe" – Spice Girls

-"You Oughta Know" – Alanis Morissette

-"Always Be My Baby" – Mariah Carey

-"California Love" – 2Pac feat. Dr. Dre

-"Breakfast at Tiffany's" – Deep Blue Something

-"No Diggity" – Blackstreet

-"Macarena" – Los Del Rio

-"1979" – The Smashing Pumpkins

-"Ironic" – Alanis Morissette

-"Name" – Goo Goo Dolls

...s from 1996

...' hadn't come out yet — it would premiere in ...r 1997.

...ould get a Big Gulp at 7-Eleven for 89 cents.

...L CDs were *everywhere* — even in cereal boxes.

...n-In was the go-to summer hair hack (whether it ...ked or not).

-Everyone watched 'Friends' on Thursday nights.

-Pizza Hut still had those red cups and Book It! rewards.

-People called their friends from cordless phones — or payphones!

-Tamagotchis were banned in some schools.

-Beanie Babies were starting their world takeover.

-Columbia House offered 12 CDs for a penny (and haunted you for years after).

-Sun-In

-Lip Smackers

-Aussie Hair Gel

Snacks & Sips We Loved

- Snapple Elements
- Capri Sun
- Fruit by the Foot
- Dunkaroos

- Lunchables
- Gushers
- Pepsi Blue
- Trix Yogurt

What We Played
- Tamagotchis
- Skip-It
- Super Nintendo
- Game Boy Color

School Supplies That Slayed
- Lisa Frank
- Scented Gel Pens
- Trapper Keeper
- Glitter Glue
- Snap Bracelets

Top Movies/TV Shows from Summer '96:
-Clueless (on VHS, taped from HBO)-Party of Five, Friends, Beverly Hills, 90210-Space Jam promos starting to pop up-Titanic was still a rumor...

The Summer I Met My Mom: The Mixtape
(Now streaming in your heart—and maybe on Spotify)

- "Wannabe" — Spice Girls
- "Give Me One Reason" — Tracy Chapman
- "Where Do You Go" — No Mercy
- "I'll Be There for You" — The Rembrandts
- "Kiss Me" — Sixpence None the Richer
- "Macarena" — Los Del Rio
- "Say You'll Be There" — Spice Girls
- "Because You Loved Me" — Celine Dion
- "California Love" — 2Pac feat. Dr. Dre
- "Always Be My Baby" — Mariah Carey

Author's Note

If you were a teen in 1996, I hope this brought you back. And if you weren't? Welcome to a world of butterfly clips, Walkmans, and big dreams.

xo, K.S. DeLuca